For Portulak and Pastinake

Original title: DER BLUMENBALL
Copyright ©2005 Annette Betz Verlag im Verlag Carl Ueberreuter, Vienna – Munich
English Text ©2005 Philip Boehm

The Flower Ball / Sigrid Laube / Silke Leffler
Summary: The story of acceptance, the merging of poetry and the world of plants

ISBN-13: 978-0-9646010-2-4
ISBN-10: 0-9646010-2-8

Library of Congress Catalog Card Number: 2005928834

10 9 8 7 6 5 4 3 2

Design: Peri Poloni, Knockout Design, www.knockoutbooks.com

Published by Pumpkin House, Ltd
P.O. Box 21373
Columbus, Ohio 43221
www.pumpkinhouse.com

Printed in Singapore

The Flower Ball

By Sigrid Laube

Illustrated by Silke Leffler

English text by Philip Boehm

Pumpkin House

"Tonight," proclaimed Cauliflower, "I shall attend the Flower Ball. Who would like to come along?"

Onion crinkled in dismay. "The *Flower Ball?* But what about our Vegetable Bunch — that's much more fun!"

"You should stick with your own kind," Lettuce scolded. "Everything has its place, and this is where you belong."

"Proper vegetables never look past their own fence!" chirped the Radishes.

Cucumber nodded sagely in agreement. "Beware the flowers across the garden border," she warned. "They're snobby and snooty and look down their noses at us, those stuck-up vase stuffers!"

"Better not to have anything to do with them," snapped the Peas, shaking and rattling inside their pods. "Those fancy-pansies, those fluff-puffs, those ornamental dandies...."

"What do all of you have against flowers?" sighed Cauliflower sadly. "I'd like to go to their ball, but I don't dare go alone."

"I don't have anything against flowers. They just look different and sometimes they don't smell as good as we do," Carrot sighed. For a moment she was silent.

Then she made a decision: "You know what?" she declared with trembling tuber. "I'll go with you!"

"Magnificent!" Cauliflower spruced up his leaves and topped off his outfit with an airy feather, while Carrot donned a beautiful mask.

"You look so nice, the two of you!" whispered the Radishes, suddenly embarrassed by their own red cheeks.

Cauliflower puffed out his chest and offered Carrot his strong right arm.

"May I have the pleasure, Mademoiselle?"

She gave a cheerful nod and together they skipped lightly out of the vegetable patch.

to the Flower Ball

Vegetable Bunch

Il Ballo dei Fiori

The ball was already in full swing. The flowers had asked the
Roosters, the Chickens and the Pussy Willows to help out. The
Crickets were trilling away in fine spirits, while the Sparrows
chirped a jazzy backbeat. Someone had drilled a hole in the rain
barrel, and Beetle was serving up the bubbly water.

Barnyard Dog wagged them through the gate.

Cauliflower and Carrot strolled on in, smiling this way and that.

"And who might *they* be?" whispered Carnation to an older Tulip, who peered over her glasses and wrinkled her nose.

"It appears that some vegetables have decided to crash our party."

Carnation was so shaken she ruffled her petals.

"Oh my!" she exclaimed. "Raw vegetables — how dreadfully crude!"

   "What are they doing here, anyway? Do they even have an invitation?" asked Rose.

   "A pretty plain-looking pair, don't you agree, my love?" Lavender bowed stiffly to his Lady Rose and led her onto the dance floor. She was still young and glowing.

"We ought to throw them out. The idea of some perfectly strange vegetables showing up at our ball, just like that — whoever heard of such a thing?" Larkspur bristled ferociously.

"Miserable groundlings, wretched undergrowth!"

"You're absolutely right! They're nothing but tedious soup-wallowers!" Marigold wilted with disgust.

Cauliflower heard the mumbling and grumbling; he saw that the Roses were quivering and that the Carnations were shivering, all in a huff. Pansy even got the hiccups.

"Something tells me they don't like us," Cauliflower said to Carrot.

"That's a pity because their music is sooo beautiful," Carrot sighed dreamily. Then she thought a moment. "Have we done something to them?" she asked Cauliflower.

"No. Have they done anything to us?" he asked back.

"No," replied Carrot.

"In that case there's no reason for anyone to be angry," declared Cauliflower, relieved. He smoothed out his feather and bowed to Carrot.

"May I be so bold, my lady?" he said. "Would you care to dance?"

Carrot was delighted: after all, the night was balmy, the light was soft, and the Lightning Bugs were in fine spirits. The moon rolled up into the sky and stars came peeking out, full of curiosity.

Carrot winked through her mask at Cauliflower, and held out a tender leaf: "It would be a pleasure."

They mingled among the dancers. Elegant Phlox shrank away from them, and they stepped on Clematis' toes.

"If at least they were weeds," groaned Wisteria. "After all, weeds bloom almost like we-" she stopped in mid-sentence.

Cauliflower had wrapped his arms around Carrot's waist and was dancing a snazzy Snap-Bean Rumba. Then he led her through a breezy Cucumber Tango, and finally the two vegetables frisked out a spicy Chili-Pepper Cha-Cha-Cha. Carrot lost her breath but bravely followed her partner and didn't once lose her footing. They were a beautiful sight and the flowers couldn't help but applaud.

After that Pussy Willow ventured to approach Carrot, and Cauliflower asked Marigold to join him for a charming waltz. Next he danced a galop with Salvia and a jaunty polka with Lily.

It turned out to be a grand evening. Everyone got to know Carrot and Cauliflower and they all learned that they could get along splendidly.

"We'll have you over to our Vegetable Bunch," promised Cauliflower in parting.

"And you'll be sure to come to our next ball, won't you?" asked Lavender eagerly — he was somewhat taken by Carrot.

The two vegetables tiptoed back home. They were very happy and very tired and didn't want to wake anybody up.

Just as Cauliflower was falling asleep, he whispered: "Who would have thought it? I have to write down everything that happened tonight, so I will never forget it."

"I will draw some pictures for you," Carrot whispered back. "That way we'll have a book."

Her eyes closed. "And someday we'll read it out loud to our grandchildren!" And soon she was gently snoring.